Clint Faraday
book forty four
A Bloody Shame

The regular group sitting in The Golden Grill are discussing the way a local con man had stolen the life savings of a resident from England. They are talking about how the corrupt court system will let him get away with it.

Roland Eggars, himself a Britisher, says the way those people were able to manipulate the judges and police was a bloody shame. Sooner or later someone would come along and put an end to some of their practices.

It was sooner.

Contents

About the author

CD Moulton has traveled extensively over much of the world both in the music business, where he was a rock guitarist, songwriter and arranger and in an import/export business. He has been everything from a bar owner to auto salvage (junkyard) manager, longshoreman to high steel worker, orchid grower to landscaper, tropical fish farmer to commercial fisherman. He started writing books in 1983 and has published more than 350 books as of January 1, 2023. His most popular books to date are about research with orchids, though much of his science fiction and fantasy work has proven popular. He wrote the CD Grimes, PI series, and the Det. Nick Storie series, Clint Faraday series, and many other works.

He now resides in Gualaca, Chiriqui, Panamá, where he writes books, plays music with friends, does research with orchids and medicinal plants. He has lately become involved in fighting for the rights of the indigenous people, who are among his closest friends, and in fighting the extreme corruption in the courts and police in Panamá.

He offers the free e-book, *Fading Paradise*, that explains what he has been through because of the corruption.

CD is the discoverer of the Chadam Protocol for curing cancer.

Facebook page Ambrosia peruviana for cancer.

A Bloody Shame

<u>*Regular Gossip Session*</u>

"You heard about what that bunch of crooks in David did to Henry Johnson, didn't you?" Jim asked of the regular group who sat in the Golden Grill for coffee and gossip, most days.

"Yes. They wiped him out for the most part," Tom, asshole of the group (in Clint Faraday's opinion), said, leaning back and getting a pious look on his face. "I warned him about letting those people get to him. I told him he stood to lose everything he had saved up to retire here. He wouldn't listen. Everybody thinks they can beat the corrupt system here, but they never can. It's too entrenched. I told him ten times to be careful, but, oh, no, he knew what he was doing.

"You see what happens to people who won't listen to advice from people who know."

Roland Eggars, newest regular member of the group, said, "You told him? I don't think I heard that. Henry was with me every time we came to Bocas Town. I don't recall him ever speaking with you."

"Er, well, uh, it was one day when I was down by the ferry dock. He was waiting for something to come over from Almirante or something and we talked. Pondres was talking to him and I spoke with him for a few minutes when he left."

"You told him ten times in a few minutes?" Roland asked, innocently. Jim burst out laughing.

"Dave had the same thing happen to him," Carl said, quickly. He didn't want any confrontations started. "After it was done, fifty people said they could have warned him about those crooks. He asked why they didn't, then. They didn't have an answer."

"Well, whatever. It's a bloody shame that those people can get away with that kind of thing," Eggars replied. "If anyone had told Henry about them he would have investigated. Since they stole his entire retirement a lot of people said the same thing. They could have told him about those crooks. The point is, *no* one did. He would have investigated."

"Always a day late," Jim agreed. "I suppose I could have warned him, but I never knew he was dealing with them. We only spoke the two times here. You were with him."

"It's the way in all of Central America," Joe said. "The corruption is ridiculous.

"I imagine it's as bad in the states and England.

They're more subtle is all. Here, it's just plain blatant. Everyone from the gas man to the top is on the take."

"Yes. It's a bloody shame the courts and police can get away with it for year after year and all the politicians do about it is promise to stop it," Eggars agreed. "It's bloody sickening. It hurts the whole country. People are becoming afraid to buy anything here. Sooner or later someone is going to come along who *will* do something about it."

"Can't be soon enough for me!" Jim replied. "The only way is to clean house completely. It's not going to happen. The next crop would take all of two seconds to become as corrupt as the ones they replaced."

"They need a machine to run things the way Dave wrote in that *Flight of the Maita* series," Bill said. "I mean, it's true what he said. How do you corrupt a machine? The programmer may be a piece of shit, but the machine could be made to do the job without ... it's like he says. When have you ever heard of a machine wanting something? There isn't any such thing as a greedy machine, only greedy designers of machines."

"He also points out that there would be exact justice. We can never allow that. We want mercy along with justice," Tom said. "That science fiction stuff is naive and juvenile. I could write something a lot more realistic than that garbage. I could design a governing system that would cut the corruption out right now! Maybe I'll write a book about it!"

"I'm sure there's nothing beyond your ability," Eggars said, sourly. "You did write a book. You never shut up about it – or didn't before Dave marched you to the internet and Googled your book. It was a vanity press? You *paid* them to publish it?

"Dave has more than a hundred fifty books published now. He didn't pay anyone anything to publish them. I've read some of the Maita books. I can see how it would work, but you'd have to build an intelligent machine. That's the problem with the theory."

"Yeah! The whole problem is that an intelligent machine *would* want something and wouldn't change anything!" Tom spat.

"That's ridiculous!" Carl said.

"Let's not get into that kind of thing here," Jim warned. "It only gets tempers up. We can talk about the fishing or something. Tuna are running out of the Zapitillas."

They talked about other things the rest of the morning.

"A news note: Judge Tremania, of Chiriqui,

under investigation for corruption, was found dead in the kitchen of his residence this morning when Teresa Gonzales, his maid, came to work. She said that there was blood all over. Police are investigating. TVN will bring all information to you as soon as it is known.

"In other news, the protest of the fishermen..."

Clint Faraday, retired PI from Florida, now living in Panamá, shook his head and asked his beautiful wife, Tyna, "Where is Dave?"

She laughed. "It wasn't Dave. She said it was bloody. Dave wouldn't make a mess."

Their son and daughter, Nito and Nicole, came in and climbed onto Clint, who was laying in a hammock on the porch of the house they were renting in Soloy, comarca Ngobe Bugle, Panamá. Clint had the honor of being the second white person to be declared a Ngobe Indio by the ruling council. Tyna was Ngobe and his children were being raised in the Indio tradition. They were in Soloy only because the school in Quebrada Tula wasn't finished yet. It would be in less than a month. They would go there. Nito was six years old and in his first year at school. Nicole would be in the school next year officially. She was, at five years old, auditing the classes Nito was attending. Tyna had taught them both since they were less than a year old. They sometimes sounded almost like adults from the time they were two and three years old.

They weren't running around the house nude like in Tula, Cusapín or Bocas Town. Clint had always waited until after he decided what he was going to do on a given day to dress. Only Tyna insisted on wearing clothes in the house early in the morning.

Tyna brought some hojaldres and bolitas and coffee for Clint and same, minus the coffee, for Nito and Nicole. They got fresh pineapple/ banana chicha.

"Noticias especiales!" came on the TV. "A second judge was found murdered this morning! Judge Renaldo Hernandez, also under investigation for corruption, was found dead in the kitchen of his home when his driver went to take him to the judicial. This is the second judge found murdered this morning. Both killings were described as very bloody. TVN will bring you information as rapidly as it is obtained."

"Now *I* want to know where Dave is!" Tyna cried.

"He's in Cusapín," Nicole answered. "Gloria talked with me on the celular last night and he was there."

"I wasn't serious," Tyna said. "It's just that Dave was put through unmitigated hell by that corrupt bunch in David."

About ten minutes later the story came on the news. " ... Both judges were tortured. Police were looking into who had made threats against ... a moment ... Noticias especiales! Policia Capitan Ramondo Morales has been found dead in the kitchen of his home. It is another bloody scene. Morales was implicated in the corruption charges with the two dead judges and four other persons. TVN will bring you any new information as soon as it is obtained."

"This is getting out of hand!" Clint exclaimed. "Those were three of the crooks Dave has filed denunciados against! He's filed against seven people directly and a *bunch* more indirectly. If any more of them end up dead he'll definitely be investigated!"

"He's in Cusapín," Nito said.

"But it's damned easy to hire a hit man here."

"As Dave says, 'There's that!'" Nito replied.

Half an hour later a fiscalía officer was found dead. He was found tortured to death in a pool of blood in his kitchen.

"I think I'd better go to David. Lucky we're so close," Clint said. "You know they're going to go after Dave. He's made charges against a lot of them."

"I was going to suggest it," Tyna replied.

Clint arrived in David three hours later. He drove directly to the main police station and to the office of Tonio Ramirez, jefe of the violent crimes department. He had worked with Tonio several times and knew him to be a good, honest cop.

"What about those judges and such?" Clint asked as he came into Tonio's office.

"Where's your friend, Dave?" he replied. "If it's him, I'll show him how to not make such a mess when he offs that whole bunch. Do you know how hard it is to work when there's sticky blood everywhere?"

"I tend to agree. That's why I know it's not Dave."

"I know it's not Dave, but he'll know who it *is* probably."

"I don't think so. He would handle it himself. I do know he has a way. He wouldn't torture them – except one. He thinks they should just be gotten rid of. Torture doesn't solve anything."

"It might make others think about it before they get involved with ... nah! Ain't gonna happen."

"Who's the latest to file charges against that

bunch of sleazeballs those corrupt pieces of shit are protecting?"

Tonio pointed to a pile of files on his desk. "That's for the past five years." There were nine files. Clint put Dave's aside. He knew that one intimately.

Tomas Baskins – Boquete

Mary Ann Downs – returned Texas

James LeFlor – returned France

Conrad Hennessy – Costa Rica

Phillip Conners – PC

Arnold Fadigan – returned Ireland

Jaques Vilon – Boqueron

Henry Johnson – Bocas del Toro

He read the older files first. Baskins had a heart condition. He was out of it so far as Clint was concerned.

Downs was out of it. She wasn't here. Ditto LeFlor and Fadigan.

Hennessy could come from Costa Rica in an hour. He was in it. Conners was in Panamá City. He could be in Chiriqui at any time. That was his residence, not where he was at a given moment.

Vilon was residing in Boqueron. A few minutes by car. Johnson was in Bocas Province. He could be in Chiriqui in very little time.

Any of them could be staying at a hotel or with friends in David.

Zada, Tonio's new aide, came in, smiled at Clint and dropped a read-out on Tonio's desk. He picked it up, read it, sighed and handed it to Clint. "Dave did it," he declared. "He's the only one with a solid alibi and who's not in the area so he has to be it!"

Hennessy had used his passport to enter Panamá as of four days ago. Connors was supposed to be visiting with friends in Gualaca. Johnson was unknown, but his landlady in Punta Peña said he'd gone to David on a legal matter with the fiscalía. Dave was in Cusapín.

"So. Dave has a bunch of his Indio friends here to chop up that bunch with machetes," Tonio said. "I'll have to go there to question him, but I'll wait for the rest of them to get chopped up."

"Nah! It's that Mary woman!" Clint replied. "She has a nutcase cousin she hypnotized into doing it!"

"We'll have to go with LeFlor seeing as he's the farthest from here and we couldn't hope to charge him with anything at all, much less have him extradited.

"Now let's get serious. Any ideas?"

"No. This is the kind of thing I hate. Almost everyone within a thousand miles has a reason to want that bunch dead. That will mean that anyone who does have any information is *not* going to give it to us."

They discussed what seemed to be happening. The victims were literally being chopped to pieces with machetes. They didn't start in a fatal place.

"Tonio, we'd better have someone keeping an eye on the rest of those cruds. As much as I hate it, it's part of your job."

"I know. I put some regular officers on it. I can't protect 'Persons to be included at a later date' on the denunciados."

Zada came in to tell Tonio they had another. On the phone. He picked up the desk phone to say, "Ramirez here."

"Yes."

"She wasn't named, was she?"

"On the denunciados."

"Because the judges and cops killed so far were on the denunciados – or rather, they refused to act on the denunciados."

"The corruption thing."

"You are her co-worker?"

"So she was. That means we'll have to watch the earlier ones."

"Before she became the notary representative for ... some people who are pulling scams."

"Yes."

"Did you stamp any of those things?"

"Sra. Mondres, I'd advise that you go nowhere

alone until we have resolved this thing. You are probably not in any danger, but you could be."

"No. Not from them."

"Because you can testify against them. I don't mean that you are in danger from the ones who killed your boss. You're in danger from...."

"Exactly. They are facing strong prison terms. You could help convict them."

"That may be best. Be careful!"

He hung up. He wrote some quick notes, then said, "Dave had the experience that tells us they work with a crooked notary. This was another. A worker went to her house when she didn't show up for work and found her cut to pieces in the bathroom. I warned her ... well, you heard it."

Clint nodded. "It shows why you can't know who or how many to protect."

Zada came in to say that a clerk at the fiscalía was just found in the parking lot behind the wheel of his car. He was shot in the head.

"Hmm. That will be because he knew who, how and when," Tonio suggested. "Let's see if he was mentioned in any of the cases."

He went through some files, then called the fiscalía to say he wanted the files on the interviews with witnesses in those cases.

"Then I'll file some charges against you. This is a murder investigation of people in your own department if you hadn't noticed. It appears that you are hiding something corrupt, Mr. Puentes."

"Thank you. I'll expect them within the hour." He rang off and shook his head.

"The whole bunch are terrified, mostly that they'll be caught for their part. I hope they every one are!"

"We can agree on that point. I think I'll want to find who's behind this one for personal reasons. I rather doubt we'll ever get enough evidence to convict anyone."

"It's not the hired kind of thing, Clint. Whoever is doing this is personally and deeply emotionally involved."

"Yeah. Someone who's been put through the pure hell Dave went through, but someone who doesn't share his philosophy about such things. Dave would probably just shoot the bunch or something. He doesn't think torture accomplishes anything more than personal revenge. 'I'll put you through a few minutes of the hell you've put me through for years,' kind of thing."

"Or something else? Maybe, 'You're going to tell me who else is involved. Do it fast and die fast. Do it slow and die slow, but you *will* tell me.' That would mean we have to find who else is involved first to save them, as repulsive as the idea is to me."

"We agree on yet another point. These people are preying on the pensionados and other retired people and are taking everything they worked fifty years to get.

"I'm amazed at the difference the way I look at things has become. When I first got here it was, 'Catch the killer and let a jury decide if they deserve a stiff sentence.' Now it's more that these things are not human to me. It's like somebody's killing off the parasites in the system. They're lower than worms.

"It also saves Panamá the expense of housing and boarding them for years, as you've repeatedly stated."

"I've talked with Dave about it. I know how they operate. Getting the ones who're corrupt and working with them won't solve anything. We have to get rid of the corrupt *and* the corruptors."

"Yes. All this will do is bring in a new crop who will be less blatant about it. We can hope it results in laws to help control it."

"The laws are there. It's a matter of enforcing them. They control how, when and *if* they get enforced. It's because you've let law and the courts become big bureaucracies. That's how a bureaucracy always has and always will work. It's designed for corruption."

"It's a lot to work on. We can ... Clint, we're

sitting here trying to think of ways to make this series of torture/ murders work!"

"We're as sick as whoever's doing it is."

They gave each other the bird.

Clint looked through the papers Tonio gave him. They told him a lot and nothing. Dave had almost everything he owned in some hoods' names because he trusted one person. They used one ruse or another to get a signature, then the crooked notary to stamp that he appeared before him and read, spoke and understood Spanish. At the time he didn't speak fifty words and certainly didn't read the language.

By law, that is fraud. His case is proven. The crooked court and fiscalia have refused to act. The crooks were apparently paying them off and intimidating them. Information known only by the fiscalia was sent to them, resulting in attacks and threats. The fiscalia wouldn't even question a single witness who Dave's lawyer had brought to David to make a deposition. One judge had told the lawyer he "Wasn't interested" in Dave's case. The obvious inference was that he would get interested if he was paid enough.

Dave was fighting the corruption. He wasn't about to become part of it. He got in touch with a newspaper that claimed to be fighting this kind of thing. He was told fraud and corruption in his case, were "Personal" things.

Are they afraid of the ones behind it or are they part of it? Give me another explanation.

It was variations of that with all of them.

Clint called Dave, who said he would supply lawyers to anyone caught. He didn't know the specific individuals involved except in a few instances, but their reputation was that they were corrupt to the last one. He hadn't spoken with any but one of the people who were scammed. That one didn't have the balls to pursue it, which was exactly what the slimewads wanted.

Tonio called. A lawyer was found chopped up behind his office. He was one they had proven took money to delay investigation of two of the cases.

"If you were to kill off every crooked lawyer in David there wouldn't be five left," Clint replied. "This certainly makes it beyond reason that you would know who to protect."

"I've already let word get out that the police can only investigate the ones who are already dead. There are more corrupt officials and lawyers in David than there are police. We can't possibly protect many of them, much less all. I suggested that the killer or killers could simply watch to see who's being protected and go after others. Judge

Cedeño has demanded protection. I asked him if he was admitting to corruption. He said no. I said I didn't have the officers to protect anyone not involved. These were all people who were deeply involved in blah-blah-blah. No honest person had been harmed to my knowledge.

"He hung up. I'm going to get the word on the streets that the only way anyone involved in the corruption can hope to survive is to run or confess. Confessing might or might not work.

"There's a TV news truck out front. I'll have to talk with them. Watch TVN!" He rung off. Clint flicked on the TV and found TVN. He saw a woman at the Noticias desk. "... Policia Capitan Antonio Ramirez in a few moments. TVN is asking about this morning's rash of murders. Here is Vanesa Cortez."

The scene shifted to the front of the police station. A sexy woman with a microphone said, "Thank you, Estrella.

"I am here at the main police station where Capitan Ramirez is to explain what has happened so far in his investigations. It is now our understanding that the dead people were all named in a corruption investigation.

"Capitan Ramirez, have you made any progress in your investigation?"

"Very little, Vanesa. You have to realize that

these are all people who had been charged with corrupt acts. If there were only one or two under charges we would have a direction, people to go after. That is not the case. There are many who have charged these people with various despicable acts. Five or six, we can concentrate on. Fifteen or fifty, we have no clear direction.

"We also have the problem where one of the victims, if not more, were not killed in the same manner. The one, in particular, was shot. That smells very much like one of his co-ladrones wanted to silence him. He knew too much.

"It quickly went from someone outside taking revenge on some crooks to the crooks killing each other to garner silence. It is now a grand melee.

"The police have to concentrate on protecting the general *innocent* public. What I have to say to both sides of these killings is that involving innocent people will lead to dire consequences to all of you. Keep your gangster methods in your gangs. If it goes beyond that, it will no longer be a police matter. It will be a military matter.

"That's about it for now, Vanesa. Back to you, Estrella!" He waved and went inside. Vanesa was staring in shock. A voice from off screen said, "Vanesa?"

"Er, I didn't expect such a reaction. I don't really know how to react!"

Clint had seen what Tonio was doing. He was in an office only a few meters away. He managed to come out the door Tonio had just entered. He had given Tonio the thumbs-up when he passed him. As he stepped out, Vanesa said, "Oh! You're Clint Faraday! Are you working on this case?"

"Yes. I was asked to assist."

"Did you hear Capitan Ramirez just now?"

"Tonio? I passed him in the hallway. What did he say?"

"That he was here to protect the innocent public, not a gang of corrupt thieves, in essence. He has threatened to call in the military if they don't contain their killings inside of their gangs.

"What is your opinion of such a statement?"

"Opinion? It was honest. That really is his job, you know. To protect the innocent public.

"I am familiar with the case and with what has happened to cause this thing to happen. It was, in a way, inevitable, but corrupt people never think they'll have to answer for their acts.

"They're about to learn different. They have to consider that they each know too much for the comfort of other people who are *just like them*. That is a dangerous position to occupy.

"I really have to go, Vanesa. My only advice is for anyone with the means who was involved in the corruption to get as far away from here as is possible and as quickly as possible. There are simply too many who could be behind it. I've spent the past couple of hours in scanning over the reports these people would not investigate. The proof was obvious and there, but no action was taken. One or more of those people is taking the action themselves."

Vanesa grinned at Clint. "If everyone involved left, there wouldn't be three people left in any of those buildings. Back to you, Estrella!"

Clint went to his car and drove out as the TV truck was packing up to go.

Now to see if many of them actually would run. Vanesa had exaggerated, of course. If they all left, there would be maybe six or eight people left in those buildings. A lot of the PTJ people weren't in on it, as Dave had discovered. It was with the higher offices and the courts.

It would probably be best to wait until more was learned. Tonio asked that anyone in the judicial who hadn't called in and were late to be reported to him immediately.

Clint's phone buzzed. It was Tonio.

"Yo, Clint! Just wanted you to know that Judge Alvarado and family have decided to take a vacation in Argentina. His entire staff are free for two weeks and his cases were turned over to Macias, but he's flooded. He suggested the cases be handled by the newer judges, who all claim they aren't able to take on more at this time.

"Interesting. Delgado says he wants all the cases where complaints were filed against the system turned over to him. He guarantees the poooooor innocent victims will finally find there is justice in Panamá.

"What's he up to?"

"Maybe he's figured a way where he'll be left alone. Maybe he's sincere. I haven't ever heard of him. That's a good sign – or a very bad one."

"Bad?"

"It would mean he's the really big boys' judge. He's not heard of because he's dealing with the ones who stand to lose too much. That means they'll try to protect him at all costs."

"I see. They aren't into scamming retirees out of their life's savings. That's too petty for them."

"See if he contacts you. What he wants will tell us a lot."

Tonio agreed. Clint said he was a phone call away. He was going to talk with some people.

He found the present address of Jacques Vilon. Boqueron was closest to him. He drove to the area and found where Vilon was residing. He was surprised Vilon was home. He was invited in.

"Your friend, the botanist, Dave, he tell me about you, Clint Faraday. It is an honor. Please to enter.

"I am afraid my English, it is not good."

"Spanish is easier? I speak Spanish."

They spoke in Spanish from that point.

"You will want to know if I am a part of what is happening here. I am, in that those people have cost me my retirement savings. I have a pension that is enough to live on here, but it allows little extra. I worked for many years, now have nothing for it but mere subsistence. I desire that every one of them dies slowly and horribly. I am afraid I do not have, as you say here, the balls to do it myself."

"That's a pretty general consensus. They aren't popular people."

"I hope also that the ones who are directly doing those things will die as slowly and as horribly."

"We agree there, also. Do you know who's behind it?"

"No. If I did, I would not tell you. I would not tell anyone."

They discussed Vilon's case. It was a matter of a crooked lawyer who had him sign a power of attorney, then had "sold" his land to another lawyer. Four lawyers later, each one claiming to be working on the case, he got one that actually did. It went to the fiscalia where no action was taken, no witnesses' statements were taken, no investigation was ever started. It was more than two years of non-action by the court system.

"There's a judge who claims that he's going to review every single complaint and you'll find justice."

"Delgado? He's superior. He refused to review them before, but he will now? What a thrill!"

Clint called Tonio to tell him what Vilon said, then Vilon told him.

"Clint, he's told Vanesa, the TVN reporter, he wants a meeting with me to keep our departments working together."

"Yes! Call her! Agree! Say the meeting will be public under the auspices of transparencia! She can be there and can even be asked to moderate if things get heated!"

There was a silence. He could picture the evil grin that soon came across Tonio's face.

"What a good public-spirited idea! I'll call her now. You get back here as fast as you can." He rung off.

"Will that solve anything?" Vilon asked.

"Yes! If he makes a statement on TV he can't back out of it. He could claim your cases were incomplete or something on that end, but not if Tonio points out some things from the first. He's now forced to see that your property's returned, if not more."

"You are a friend. I think if I knew I would tell you. You would at the worst have use of the information, just too late to act upon it."

"Something like that. A day late and a Balboa short!"

They shook hands and Clint headed back to David as fast as he dared. Tonio called and said for him to go directly to the Ciudad Judicial.

"What we have to accomplish is a correlation of data between the police and the courts. It will guarantee oversight," Delgado intoned, striking a pose. "I have long decried the lack of such a system. We have to know what you are doing to know how to act."

"We are doing what we swore to do when we took our jobs. We're acting in the interest of the public security and protection," Tonio replied. "What we are concerned with here is what you are doing in the courts. Or not doing."

"I am acting as quickly as I can to rectify the scurrilous acts of a couple of my fellow judges. I intend to see that the public is given all the...."

"If you gentlemen will both drop the political speeches and get to the matter at hand, I'm sure our audience will appreciate it," Vanesa said, shortly. Tonio had told her to come down equally on both of them. He would try to supply reason for his chastisement. He was positive Delgado would supply his own.

"Sorry. It's a habit," Tonio replied. Delgado reddened and said that was true of anyone in their positions.

"I don't exactly know how to proceed here," Delgado announced. "In the court witnesses and evidence are presented and questions are asked. It is to the judge to decide what is pertinent from the evidence introduced. It is a long-used process to avoid the court being tied up with frivolous cases. We act only upon the evidence presented. We can't act on evidence not presented. It is that simple."

"That's partly true," Tonio said, quickly. "There are points in the law about which evidence is pertinent where it is not – or it shouldn't be – the decision of the judge to consider.

"We can use a modified system much like that. The difference here will be that evidence that is covered under the law can't be excluded."

"I'm sure I don't know to what you refer, but I can and do accept the concept. Perhaps you will clarify?"

"Yes. I can site one example from my head. It isn't necessary to look it up. I've studied all the complaints a little. A very common thing in them is that a contract was presented to the court that was in Spanish, but the declared signer of the contract did not speak or read Spanish. There was no translation provided to that signer.

"By law, that is fraud. The case was won at that point, but your courts and the fiscalia did not in any case consider that fact. Five of the cases were non-cases and needed only the court's agreement that it was fraud. The perpetrators of that fraud were not prosecuted.

"Sr. Delgado, that is not acceptable. Retired people are being cheated and robbed of their life's savings by these ladrones. The court does nothing. It does not follow the laws you have sworn an oath to follow. There is no other way to see it. Panamá is getting a very bad international reputation for this corruption. It must stop.

"It was stated several times that continuance of this process has an inevitable end. We've reached that end.

"Had you, and that is not a personal 'you,' done as you have sworn this would not be happening. If there were two or three cases we could quickly stop it. There are probably several dozen. We can't know who they are. You've brought this on yourselves.

"There is an inevitable next step. Whoever, singular or plural, is or are doing this will most certainly next go after the corruptors. First stop the corrupt, then stop those who sponsor that corruption. All history warns of this. All of you refuse to look at that history the same way you refuse to look at the evidence presented."

Delgado stood and walked out.

"Back to you, Vanesa!" Tonio said. Vanesa grinned. "I think the judge made a very clear statement, don't you? Back to you, Estrela!"

The audience applauded. Long and loud.

"We now have a war between the police and courts," Tonio warned, quietly. "I think it will mainly be here in Chiriqui. The national system will have to step in now.

"Clint, tell Dave and all the others to lay very low until this balances as much as it will. This won't stop anything for more than a few days, but it'll make them more careful."

Clint nodded and looked grim. "I think you may have given them an idea they didn't have at first. About the sleazeballs who were working the scams."

"I hope so. I just hope they realize they will be going after some hardened people with centuries of experience, not a few crooked judges and cops."

Vanesa asked Tonio if he would object to answering a couple of questions. He didn't really have a way out, so agreed. They brought a camera and a microphone.

"Capitan Ramirez, that was some show. Judge Delgado made a statement it would be hard to not understand when he walked out. The meeting was at his suggestion. Why did you come down so hard on him?"

"I came here to discuss a real and immediate problem. He opened the meeting with a typical political speech that was a lot of words to say nothing. I'm afraid that this case is wearing the department and myself down. You might say he pushed the wrong 'start' button at the wrong time. I am tired and irritable.

"It was all too obvious he was going to put a few excuses to use later to the public, then his argument would be that the judges were never presented with the fraud evidence, making it the fault of the lawyers presenting the case.

"The lawyers are part of the corruption. They don't present that. They're paid not to. In one case I have studied the lawyer made that presentation, but the judge refused to consider it as evidence.

"Next, all the court would have to do is demand a copy of a certified payment or a notarized receipt. No lawyer anywhere will hand a person thousands of dollars and not get a receipt. In none of these cases was a receipt mentioned. It is a second point where the case was won before it was presented to the court. By established law!

"The courts did not even question a single witness? Did not ask for a receipt? Did not consider that it is, by law, proven fraud?

"I have investigated many cases. In some earlier cases against these same people a person, usually an Indigeno, was actually killed and false papers presented that the courts upheld! You heard a lot about it from the Wild Bill case. You heard nothing of it from the cases of the death of an Indio or ten.In my personal opinion, each of those judges, lawyers, investigators, whether police or other, are guilty of conspiracy to commit murder! They are all accomplices to murder!"

"Well! You seem to have answered all my questions at once! Thank you, Capitan Ramirez.

"Back to the studio."

Tonio waved for Clint to come with him. They went to the parking lot to talk. Reporters from the local and national newspapers converged on them. Tonio called for silence, then said, "I said almost everything I have to say inside. I am tired and there are still a lot of killings out there to solve. That's my job now. I'll appoint an aide, Srgnta. Zada Hernandez, to keep all of you apprised of what is happening. Distractions such as this delay solution and accomplish little else."

"You are required to answer our questions! By

law!" one of them called.

"No I'm not. I'm required to tell you what is in public domain – and not me. Whoever I appoint. This is an investigation in progress and I don't have to tell you shit! *By law*! I can appoint the boy who carries lunches to prisoners or Zada. At my discretion. Anymore silly demands and it's Roberto. Got it?"

The other reporters applauded. One asked if he could have just one question answered. Tonio nodded.

"Are you really going to call in the military?"

"I can't call in the military, but I can request the president send troops here to protect the public. I won't hesitate if anyone who is innocent becomes endangered."

They filed away and Tonio called Zada to tell her she was the contact with reporters. She knew what to tell them.

"What?"

"How many did you say?"

"I'll get on it." He rang off.

"Four lawyers in one of the most corrupt firms in the country seem to have had an accident. They got in their car at a restaurant and it exploded."

"So! Someone else has gotten the idea," Clint replied.

"Yes. Different MO."

"Clint, can you tell me who's really behind this?"

"No puede! I wish I knew. They certainly have enough people with reason to want to kill off the lot of them. I think people are getting ideas and this could turn into a purge that Panamá hasn't seen in a lot of years. This one won't be political.

"Tonio, they have to go after each other while they have someone knocking them off. They get it from inside and outside."

"To tell you the truth, I can't work up any tiny bit of sympathy for any of them. They'll know exactly who to hire to hit each other. They've been protecting those people for years. One or two might have used a hit man. If so, they're really in for a ride!"

"Yeah. Victims, other scumbags and hit men, all after their slimy asses. Any others decided to take vacations in far exotic places?"

"Several. A couple are having problems in that their families don't want to go anywhere."

"I hope it doesn't get to the point where anyone goes after the families."

"How very true. Then we have to get in deep whether we want to or not."

Clint nodded. They got in their cars and went their separate ways. Clint called Tyna and talked for a half hour. Manuel Silva, an Indigeno court officer, tried to come to the comarca and the council expelled him. They said he had disgraced every Ngobe and would not be protected by them. He went on back and they thought he was going to Darien.

He had gotten three call attempts while he was talking with Tyna and called Tonio back.

"Clint? Judge Fonzinni has turned himself in. He'll give testimony about some others if we protect him."

"Expected. A couple of them."

"Clint! We can't protect him! Where will we take him? How can we protect him when there are some police officers higher up involved in the corruption gang? They have to see he's not protected!"

"Tonio! You and Zada keep him in your office! I'll be right there!"

"I can tell by your voice that you have an idea. We'll keep him here. Fast, Clint!"

Clint left the restaurant and headed for the station. He had an idea, all right!

"Put him in cell S four A," Tonio ordered two hours later. "That's secure and isolated."

The officers and Zada marched Fonzinni off. Tonio looked at Clint, who nodded the least bit.

"Well, we might get a break," Tonio said to the four lawyers and two other police officers still in the office. "We can protect him for a little while. As soon as they learn where he is we'll have to move him."

Lico. Alvarez started, "Well! We can hope this one will give us some insight into the way...."

"Can it!" Clint demanded. "There aren't any reporters here and you're downright obsequious with that crap!

"Tonio, we have to find a way to get him to Panamá City or somewhere. There's a better chance of protecting him there. He can't give us anything new, but he can confirm, legally, what we know.

"Try to get him transferred after midnight. I know how to get him out. That will be the safest time. The only cars on the road will be easy to watch. We can send out a decoy first. The real transport will be ten minutes later."

"Let's not divulge our plan here," Tonio warned, sternly. "Shall we break this up? I'm hungry and tired."

They filed out. Clint and Tonio went to La

Tipica, not far from the station. They sat to have a meal and to talk.

"It's set up?" Tonio asked.

"Yeah. There's that hallway, twenty four feet, before the cell. The only other door there is to the storage room. I have cameras and video-recorders that don't miss an inch. I also have the detectors in place. Fonzinni is in Zada's apartment. Lilia, her landlady, will keep anyone out of there."

They got back to the station. Two lawyers were abducted at gunpoint by four masked men. Their bodies were found fifteen minutes later by a little drainage creek. A court aide who had a reputation of getting private appointments with judges and police department heads was cut to pieces. No less than three other judges were shot at, one was hit in the crotch. Tonio grinned at that. He was known to make deals with young women to get them off on minor charges. "One of them wants to see the particular practice does not continue," Tonio suggested.

They went to the judicial. There was almost no one on the property.

Tonio got a call. "Already!" he cried. "We'll be right there!"

Clint asked if there was already an attempt on Fonzinni.

"It looks very possible. We have to ask some

questions of a young cop."

They walked into the station and the guard said he was wanted in his office. He thanked him and he and Clint went in to find Zada had a trainee officer handcuffed to the ring on the wall.

"Details," Tonio said.

"Trainee Beto Morales Smith. Working here three days. Off duty. He was seen in the hall, earlier, but he only went in a meter or so, then back out. He waited in the baño for a few minutes, then went back into the hall and stayed very close to the wall. He went to the door and tried the knob. It turned and he went very quickly and silently back to the baño. He waited a few minutes, then went back to the hallway and to the outer door. He went inside. Flores was on the bunk with his back to the entrance, pretending to be asleep.

"He then took a thin steel wire from his pocket and went silently to the cell and was reaching in to place the wire around Flores' neck when we grabbed him."

"Good work!

"Well, Trainee Morales, what do you have that you *will* tell us?"

"I want to talk with a lawyer! I won't answer any questions without a lawyer!"

"No lawyer in his right mind would come here

for you with what's happening! If anyone comes, it'll be someone like you. Someone who is to silence you."

Morales looked lost and terrified. He shook his head.

"Very well. Zada, take him to general and lock him in."

"General?! But ... they have ... but ... please! Not general!"

"It won't make a difference. Fonzinni isn't in general," Clint pointed out.

"I'm dead! Oh, god! I'm dead!"

"Give us a name. I'll arrange for you to be taken to another jail. They won't know which one," Tonio said.

"That lawyer. At the meeting. I think he's called Alvarez. I don't know if that's his first or second apelido."

"How were you contacted?" Clint asked.

"He talked to me here. By the reception desk."

"What did he say? As close as you can tell me."

"That a client of his would pay me ten thousand dollars if Judge Fonzinni had a fatal accident or something."

"Did he give you an advance – and how did he know you were open for this kind of thing?"

"He gave me five hundred. I did some work for a man he works for. I got in trouble and Fonzinni was going to go after me until Na-nuh ... my boss stopped him."

They made arrangements for Morales to be taken to Horconcitos. That was an easier place to defend. Clint and Tonio went to call on a lawyer.

"Mr. Alvarez, we haven't time or patience to go on with this. You can give us your client or you can go down for the hard one. It won't be here. This is now handled in The City."

"I don't know what you're talking about! You can't come in here and threaten me!"

"Shit!" Clint snapped. "Alvarez, how would you take the news that everything said within three meters of the reception desk at the station is recorded in sound as well as on the camera?"

"*Er!?*"

"We can either walk out of here congratulating each other or we can take you out in handcuffs. Think about it!" Tonio said.

Alvarez sat back and was deeply thoughtful for a minute. "If you go out there acting like I told you anything, I will be dead before dinnertime. If you take me out like I've been arrested, they will assume that you couldn't make me say anything. I can have my associates come to the station and I will come back here with them, joking and laughing about the stupid police. They will assume they are safe where I am concerned.

"Do you know who I have to refuse to name?"

"Morales worked for him. He had trouble with Fonzinni and Fonzinni was paid to drop it."

"Fonzinni is cheap! It's easier to let him think what will happen if he doesn't cooperate. I imagine every lawyer who works David will lose his – or her – license over this.

"You know it was Donando De La Cruz. I didn't tell you anything actually. This is a lever I can use to get consideration?"

"To a point. You still have to survive until we can stop it. You'll be watched by the corrupt and stalked by the victims. I can try to protect you, but it will be safer for you if I'm not known to be doing that."

"I'm not concerned with that. I'm working only among them. They know I have what is called insurance.

"I swear to you, I do not, ever, allow myself to be used to harm who you have described as the innocent public, though a great number more than you suspect are far from innocent.

"My fear is from the victims who have started this. They have nothing to lose if they kill me. The other side has more than you can conceive to lose!

"I have appointments in about an hour. If you could perhaps arrest me now so that I may be back here before then?"

They stood. Tonio wrapped a Cable-Tie around Avarez's wrists. Clint messed up his hair and yanked his coat to the side, then kicked over the trash can and knocked some things off the desk. They roughly marched him out. He yelled for Tomas to get to the central station and get him out! Now!

They drove to the station. Tomas was there less than two minutes later. He was yelling about police brutality and disrespect (!) of honest citizens.

They went inside where Zada and Tonio gave Tomas a hard time. Clint acted like he was questioning Alvarez just out of hearing. He was getting louder and louder and seemed to be getting madder and madder while Alvarez was smirking and claiming there would be charges against the police and the city. Zada came over and talked to Clint quietly. Clint stormed out of the room. Zada said she was going to take it on her own authority to allow Alvarez to go, but he remained under arrest.

"Mr. Alvarez, we don't have direct proof. We have reliable witnesses and we have the person who you hired. He will break down. You will be charged with accessory to conspire to commit murder. You will serve six to ten years.

"Do not attempt to leave the city. That will be flight to avoid prosecution and will prove our case without further evidence.

"In other words, get the fuck out of this station so we can bring in the decontamination crew! Try to run and you'll be shot as an escapee, got it?"

She cut the Cable-Ties and Tomas and Alvarez slammed out. They managed to stay where the two or three loitering around could see them and hear snatches.

Clint came back in and demanded to know why that sleazeball bastard son of a bitch was walking away. Zada said he was an assistant to the police, not the police, so get off his high horse or she would knock him off of it.

He apologized as they walked back through the outer room. He said the shithead got to him. He was usually more reasonable. He never wanted to smack some asshole turkey in the puss like he wanted to smack that one!

They went to Tonio's office. Dave was sitting there. Clint thought he'd glimpsed him in the outer room during the Alvarez caper.

"Pretty good act. I don't think they'll tumble to the fact you rolled him over.

"So! Who's behind it?"

"On the perpetrator end, Donando De La Cruz. On the victim retaliation end we don't have a clue," Clint replied. "On the judges' end, about six of them."

"That all? I'll try to find out who's behind my end. I won't tell you. I'll probably offer help. If you catch anyone, I'll write an opinion whereunder a person has a right to defend himself and seek return of stolen property when the state refuses to enforce the law on the books, making the courts criminals – by definition."

"Criminals? I agree, but what's the argument the public will accept?"

"They each and every one swore a solemn oath to uphold the law. They then refused to do so, making them perjurers. In cases where there have been deaths or extreme violence, perjury gets you four to six years."

"Studied the law, did you? They're so confused not even the judges can untangle them," Tonio said, with a grim grin.

"To a purpose, but these laws aren't ambiguous. Certain areas are fairly clear."

"The law's very clear," Tonio said to the press conference. "This started out as an investigation into killings of judges and has come full circle to discovery of excesses and truly criminal acts by some of those judges."

"When you have to file charges through their own corrupt courts you're on a big round track to nowhere, and we all know it!" a reporter yelled. "The only ones who'll be charged with anything are the ones who're dead! They'll claim that's all who were corrupt! Back to business as usual!"

"Do you think it's about over?" another called.

"We can't possibly say. We can't know with any real certainty which ones are corrupt and who whoever is doing that part will go after," Zada replied. "One judge knows he is a target and has turned himself in. He knows, as do we all, that is the only way he can find protection. Any other who has the intelligence to see his or her only chance of survival is to confess and...."

"Capitan Ramirez! Capitan Ramirez! Donando De La Cruz was just shot by a sniper!" an officer yelled, coming out of the station on the run.

"Meeting adjourned!" Zada cried. They all raced back inside the police station.

"Details!" Tonio demanded.

"All I know is that Officer Juarez, who was surveiling De La Cruz, called to say De La Cruz and two local hoods were meeting by his car. They had just exchanged what is a suitcase full of hundred dollar bills that De La Cruz brought for one with gold and silver bars. The two locals were also shot. Gordo Santo and Pablo Torres.

"Do they know where the shots came from?" Clint asked.

"No. It's a puzzle. There's nowhere close and it's not possible to say where the shots came from."

Oh, shit! Dave! No! Clint thought. He slipped into a side room and called Dave, who said he wasn't involved and he didn't give his invention to anyone.

Clint went back out. Tonio raised an eyebrow. Clint said Dave was not involved. Tonio and Clint were the only two besides a small number of Indios who knew about the invention.

They went to the scene. Clint stood where each body was laying and looked for where the shots might have come from. The bodies definitely dropped immediately. They were shot through the head. Very centered shots just above the ear.

He had a one eighty field to search. There was a concrete block wall to one side.

Clint checked the wall and found three impact holes. He called over the CSI team, who said they had located the slugs. They had one already and the other two would be dug out. They were small Teflon coated slugs, probably about .300.

Clint went to each impact point and looked past where each body was laying. He had the point of origin soon, within a small area.

"This was professional." Clint announced. "The shots came from that little rise." He pointed. "It's a long way. Whoever fired those three shots that accurately has done one hell of a lot of practicing. He has a scope with a range-finder that had to cost five grand itself. I haven't heard of anyone that good in years. That's got to be eight hundred meters away, at least. Half a mile!

"We're looking for a rifle specially chambered for self-loaded extreme impact loads with a five thousand dollar scope. Either he made it himself or he paid thirty grand for the rifle. The scope will be strong enough for him to see the pores on the faces of victims a half mile away! I'll let your experts figure the muzzle velocity from that distance and that penetration. It's gonna be huge or huger!"

"So it's not the same thing as the judges?" Tonio

askcd.

"Damned if I know!"

The learned what they could at the scene and went back. Another clerk was found chopped up. A judge was beaten almost to death by a gang of people when he stopped at a market not far from his home. Two police higher-ups were missing.

They were discussing the shootings when Zada came in to say Florenzo Marin had been shot, along with a thug who was his bodyguard. They were getting in Marin's car in front of his auto repair shop (read chop shop).

"Well, they're getting rid of the worst of the worst for us. That bunch are Biblical," Tonio remarked.

"Biblical?"

"You reap what you sow. Bread on the water. Karma. They've got it coming. Collecting their reward."

"I get it already!"

Tonio looked thoughtful. He went to the file to remove the complaint files. He spent about fifteen minutes reading over them, then said, "It's part of the judge thing. Those two hoods and one other were named as the ones the fiscalia refused to investigate."

"Who's the other?" Clint asked as Zada came in. "Rosario Cesares," she said. "He was just shot coming out of Bertoni's Pizza. His lovely spouse, the real head of that bunch, went with him.

"I mean went from this world with him."

The phone buzzed and she picked it up. She said, "Zada. Habla."

"You did?"

"But we have no ... why are you admitting it?"

"I see."

"Faraday? One moment." She handed the phone to Clint.

"Clint Faraday here."

"Mr. Faraday, you were mentioned often by a mutual friend. He was scammed out of a lot of property along with several other people by the recently deceased people. A number of us have decided, seeing the police and courts refuse to act, that we will take matters into our own hands.

"I am a trained sniper. I was trained by the best. My part was getting three gangsters and their partners in crime out of the picture. I have done that and a bit more.

"My name is Hank Johnson. I am at Frontera, one step from being in Costa Rica. I think I can be in Mexico before you can stop me. They won't extradite me back to Panamá."

It was on speaker since Clint was handed the phone.

"Mr. Johnson, I am Capitan Ramirez. We have

an agreement of sorts, informal, where we don't prosecute the associates of those three who are handled by the others so long as only those few people become involved.

"I will assume that agreement extends to you so long as only they were involved. You need not leave. You have my word."

"Faraday?"

"If he says it, it's written in stone. Only he, an assistant, Zada, and I know about this conversation. It will stay that way. The Policia Nacional thanks you for your aide in getting rid of those gangster and drug ring operations in Panamá."

"That's true, but drugs?" Zada asked.

"That gold for cash was an obvious laundering of drug money," Clint replied. Tonio nodded.

"Henry, what about the others?" Clint asked.

"Among only us four?"

"Agreed, so long as it doesn't involve innocent bystanders or people who got roped into something they weren't aware of," Tonio answered.

"It doesn't. It was a thing ... what happened was that four of us who they ripped off were in Bocas making a lot of noise about our problems when an Indio who Tomas knew said he had friends who were ripped off by those same people. It started out with, 'We should get together, get a hundred Indios and all of us gringos who were ripped off and start cleaning up that crooked damned court in David.' It went from there to where we were asking if anything like that was even possible, then to making plans.

"The four Indios who had their land stolen did the chopping up bit. We all took care of at least one of the others. I'm a sniper by training and said I'd handle the mob bosses.

"The clerks, except in one incidence, were those people shutting each other up. I imagine there will be more. I understand that no one showed up for work since the announcement that it seemed to be corrupt officials and police had to cover their tails, which meant getting anyone who knows too much out of the picture. Now they have accomplices to murder added to simple corruption. It won't stop until the top one or two feel safe.

"That will tell us who was really in charge, won't it?

"I imagine one or two will be missed. It's as much as inevitable."

"What a bloody shame!" Clint said.

"You, I think I like. All three of you.

"I'm going to Mexico as planned. I'll be back. I love Panamá. That wasn't planned."

"I think the higher court will return all of your properties to you," Zada said. "If fraud was ever proven in any case anywhere in the world, it was this case and here!"

"Well, here's my ride. I hope to see all of you again. We can discuss old times. Caio!" He rung off, but not before a faint voice Clint recognized said, "Didn't I tell you?"

"Every president promises that he'll stop the corruption. None of them have been able to stop anything except in isolated cases in Panamá City. I think this will be more successful than any of the programs that try to ignore everywhere *except* Panamá City!" Tonio declared. "Maybe people will see that they can overwhelm the system with this kind of thing and stop it themselves."

"It's a bureaucracy," Clint complained. "Any bureaucracy is designed to promote corruption. The charges are filed just like here and nothing is done. The people feel impotent."

"That's because you file a complaint against the court or fiscalia with the court or fiscalia and they toss it in the nearest trash can," Zada agreed.

"There's a control board in Panamá City that investigates all these charges," Tonio argued.

"Good! Contact them and let me talk with them!" Clint cried.

"I ... let me see. They don't seem to be listed. Just a name. Junta Nacional Frente de Corupcion. No phone number or address. Hmm. No email, either."

"Oh, great! See? We have a board to control this! You have to admit that we're trying to end this *horrible* corruption problem here! See? It's right there in writing!" Clint said, dryly. "It's unfortunate that it's as much as impossible to contact them. When you do it's by telephone and they tell you the complaint must be in writing. Write it up and send it to them and they'll get right on it!

"You write. The letter is returned 'No such address.' Dave went through that. He called back and didn't get an answer. Then he learned that the phone number he had was for the director. They have a new director now. Sorry, they can't give personal information, such as how to call him.

"Fucking bullshit! It's part of the bureaucratic system to protect themselves. It's words to soothe the public."

"Which leads to the inevitable revolt by a section of the public and what we have here," Zada added.

"We'll get a new crop. They'll be as corrupt in a short time," Tonio said.

"About three minutes. I can hear Zelda yelling that there are four more dead employees at the Ciudad Judicial," Zada said. "Shall I send over Roberto, the lunch boy, to investigate?"

"We can't send anyone else. All these killings have the department swamped," Tonio answered.

Zada giggled, looked thoughtful and went out.

Clint and Tonio went to the labs to check over the evidence collected so far. They neither one wanted to find the individuals doing this. Sometimes an action that isn't legal is morally dictated as necessary.

They got back to the station an hour later as Roberto was marching a big black man into booking. Zada was almost rolling on the floor laughing. Tonio asked what was going on.

"I actually sent Roberto. I made him a special investigator. He went out there and looked over the crime scene, then went into the back employee's baño and caught Alejandro Robinson trying to get rid of a knife and gun by hiding them under the paper receptacle! The trained and experienced officers couldn't catch anyone, but the gofer in the office can!

"He said he just thought in the way a killer would think. There wasn't time from when he killed the last two until we got there for him to get out. He was covered in blood. He tried to hide the evidence. Roberto knows the type. He caught him.

"All the dead clerks worked for Tremania. They knew who was in it with him here. Somebody named Amos Puentes paid him to kill them all. There were to be two more. He was almost caught with the last one and tried to hide.

"Do you know who Amos Puentes is?"

"Isn't he that crooked asshole you said was hiding something?" Clint asked. Tonio nodded.

"Have Puentes picked up," Tonio ordered.

"They're on their way," Zada answered.

"So! We meet face-to-face!" Tonio said when they brought Puentes in. He was a nervous little mousy type. He seemed highly excited. It wasn't fear.

"Er, yes. What is the meaning of this? Those uniformed thugs came into my office and drug me out! It was humiliating. I'll file charges you may be assured!"

"Let's see. You file them with the fiscalia don't you?" Zada replied, sweetly. "We all know how far *that's* going don't we?" She winked and giggled. Puentes stared at her and reddened, then calmed down and said, "Which I will process."

"You aren't going to process anything. You're under arrest for the soliciting of at least four accomplished murders and two not completed," Tonio said.

"Charges you file with the fiscalia!" he snarled.

"Not the one here."

"It doesn't matter. I know all the people in the fiscalia. I will not be prosecuted. *I know people*!"

Clint grabbed the phone on Tonio's desk and punched a number (Tyna's). She answered and he said, "Ricardo, please. Clint Faraday calling."

"Clint? What the hell's going on?"

"Ricky Ricardo! Long time, no see!"

"Clint ...? Oh. You're conning a con."

"Yeah. That's what I'm calling about. We have a top asshole there who says he's untouchable."

"Puentes. Amos. Fiscalia. Ordered six murders, four of which happened. We have the one he hired."

"Thanks. How's the president business?"

Clint laughed. "Same old same old."

"Send him there? I suppose so. He's the creepy little crud type you want to smack in the puss. Thinks he's above the whole lot of us trailer trash."

He laughed again. "It would prove a lot cheaper for the country as well as this department."

"Will do! Ciao!"

He hung up. "Ricky says to tell you hi."

Tonio saw what Clint was doing. He hid a grin and said, "We're supposed to send him to The City?"

"He cooperates here or he cooperates there. I'd say to just send him. I don't like being in the same room with his type."

"Zada, please arrange for Sr. Puentes to be sent to main headquarters. The president requests his presence there."

"I'm to meet with President Martinelli?" Puentes asked, his eyes unnaturally bright.

"You *are* crazy!" Tonio cried. "He doesn't want to be in the same building with such as you! You're about to learn just how serious he is about breaking up this system of corruption. First hand! Clint, did he say to fly him?"

"No. Throw him in the back of the truck with the next batch, some of whom, shall we say, he was instrumental in their being in that truck."

Zada took a form from the desk and started filling it out. Clint and Tonio discussed the gangster murders. Puentes sat there, not knowing what to do. Finally he said, "I can't tolerate the humility of being sent over there as a common criminal!"

"Why not? You *are*!" Zada replied, offhandedly.

"No! I'm am *not* a common criminal! I am a planner. A very expert one!"

"So expert you and your cronies are dead or disgraced and dying. Whoopee shit!" Clint said. "Because you got away with it where you could be in control doesn't mean anything. You would be expert – if you could stay in control. Your plan would work if you could see past now.

"You failed in the long run. Now you pay the price. You'll spend the rest of your life in prison. Considering that some of the inmates are there because of your corruption I seriously doubt the rest of your life will be more than a week or so."

Puentes shut up and stared at the floor. Zada finished the form and handed it to Tonio just as Roberto opened the door. Puentes ran for the door. Roberto reacted like the street person he was and had his balled fist up when Puentes was running past. The fist and nose connected with a spurt of blood and Puentes hitting the floor.

"Hey! I didn't mean to...!" Roberto cried.

"Thank you for subduing this fleeing felon, Roberto," Zada said. "I guess this will mean we actually have to send him to Panamá City?"

"I suppose," Tonio answered. "What do you want, Roberto?"

"Jandro says he can tell you about some other things if you'll lighten up on him. I talked to him. We're both from the streets. He knows he can trust what I tell him."

"Officer Trainee Roberto, tell Jandro he will be charged with much lesser things if he cooperates fully."

"Off ... but I'm not eligible! I want ... really?"

"As capitan I can grant special consideration. I think you'll make a hell of a good cop. Report to the academy on the first, paid."

"Sir, I don't know what to say! I...!"

"Then don't say anything except that you agree.

We both have work to do here. You've done an exceptional job to date. Get back to it."

"I agree, amigo." He went out, almost dancing.

"I think he really will make a good cop," Zada said. "He likes the TV undercover cop thing. He'd be good at it!"

"Send Puentes on. Let's get some dinner."

They made out the papers to send Puentes into national jurisdiction, completely cutting off his built-in protection. Zada went out front to talk to the press, saying that the major part of the corruption scheme was defeated and that they expected a few more who could testify against the higher-ups to end up dead, but that was part of the game they were playing. They knew the rules when they joined the game.

Clint and Tonio went to Las Brasas and had a great rib-eye!

"Well, Clint. You finally get to be here with your family for a day or two!" Tyna said happily at breakfast. "You talked with Tonio on the phone for more than an hour last night. Anything new?"

"Just that another minor clerk at the judicial ended up dead and two runner-up hoods got into a gun battle trying to take over the operations of the ones knocked over by ... a friend.

"Some judges are being sent. I don't think they want to go to David, but they haven't really got a choice. A bunch of lawyers have retired just before their licenses were revoked. Several just got out of law school and have retired! What a profession! Retire at twenty two years of age!"

"You're an ass sometimes."

It was five weeks later. Clint read about the settlements in the papers and grinned at Tyna. Nito and Nicole had just left for school sign-up. They were in Quebrada Tula for just a day.

Dave called. He said he was a little hopeful about the so-called settlement, but excuse him if he didn't get excited until the papers were in his hands. There was already a delay. Announce that the courts had awarded the properties to their rightful owners, then delay after delay until someone could be bribed to 'expedite' matters. He'd gone through more than three years of that already. It was back to business as usual, if a little less blatant.

Tonio called once a week to update Clint as to what was going on in their little case. It seemed that Jandro knew a lot more than anyone guessed and had parlayed it into a suspended sentence. Roberto was now in the academy barely squeaking through on some counts, but was exceptional in others. Zada was as much as running the department, leaving him the time to investigate cases, which is what he likes. He didn't join the force to sit at a desk and tell others what to do. Puentes didn't live to reach Panamá City. He managed to commit suicide on the way. He had managed, according to the other two prisoners, to work his wrists out of the Cable-Ties and had waited until they were followed closely by a large truck. He had thrown open the door and jumped out. He hadn't taken into that consideration that he was traveling at the same speed as the truck in the same direction and had barely felt the impact. He dropped under the truck, which had jammed on the brakes, and had been run over by the rear wheels. It was a mess.

Henry Johnson was back. He had gotten to Mexico City, had hated it, and had come right back.

A man by the name of Serrano had come from Colombia and had taken over the operations of the dead gangsters. If he so much as nodded at any government employee on the streets there was a thorough investigation of that one. Panamá City had finally come to the realization that Chiriqui existed and that what happened there affected the whole country. They now had become determined that the drug traffickers weren't going to get a stronghold in David again.

Clint didn't think that would last long. The drug cartels had too much money to throw around for the political types to ignore.

Not much else. Life was back in the slow lane and things were very good for Clint Faraday and family. He hoped it would stay that way, but he hoped for a lot of things that never happened.

Clint took his family for a week in Bocas Town before the school semester started. He visited with Judi Lum, his neighbor and big help in the detective thing when in that area and partner in a foundation to build schools and clinics on the comarcas and in places where the greatest part of the population was Indio.

The second morning in Bocas Town he went to the Golden Grill to see what the latest gossip was. Henry Johnson was there. They met for the first time. They talked a little about the case. He asked Clint if they knew who had shot those gangsters. His eyes gave away that he was just having fun so Clint said, "Yes. It was done by a professional, as you probably knew. Someone with specialized training to hit that close a target from that distance. It was a way to keep those types from testifying against each other as much as anything, I suppose."

Tom had been silent so far, but couldn't resist. "I had some training in special forces with that kind of thing. They say the shots were from half a mile away. I say, 'bullshit!' The variation in wind speed and even temperature variations between the gun and target would make it as much as impossible to hit within what they described as a two inch circle on all of them. They were fired by someone no more than a quarter mile away. It was, now this is information from a very reliable source in the CIA, a CIA operation. They didn't have any other way to stop the drug trafficking there." He suddenly realized he was mouthing off in front of Clint Faraday and shut up. He'd gotten a couple of lessons about doing that!

Clint was about to say something when Henry

said, "You were in special forces? Which one?"

"Marines."

"Oh? They have something called Special Forces in the Marines?"

"Er, well, I wasn't formally in. I was sort of what you might call auditing the courses."

"They let someone audit courses for training in a top secret outfit?" Jim asked, almost laughing out loud.

"I ask because I did some work in a special unit. When was this? Where?" Henry asked.

"Er, it was back in seventy two. In Malaysia."

"Really? They were training special forces in Malaysia?"

"In the area! Not in Malaysia itself!" he cried. "I can't say anything about it! I'm sworn not to!"

"Why isn't it in your records that you were ever in the military?" Clint asked. "Why isn't it anywhere in the Malaysia area mentioned in your passport records? Why wasn't there a passport applied for by you before nineteen ninety nine?"

"It was secret work!" He was sweating. "Oh! There's Pat! Hey, Pat! I'm over here! Wait up!" He got up to almost run toward a woman who was staring at him like he was crazy. He went to her and grabbed her arm and started toward the big market. She pulled away and said something. He replied and went on across the park.

"That's the third time I've been here when he was," Henry said. "Every time he's some big-shit in some field or other. He doesn't know his prick from a cowflop!"

"We're used to him," Jim said. "He thinks he can snow anyone new. Clint slapped him down a couple of times."

"It's too bad the sniper didn't do a little extracurricular job. Him," Clint said. "Anyhow, I think things will take as much as two years to get as bad as they were if something's not put in place to stop it. You can figure the chances of that ever happening."

"With the wind flow modular and temperature inversion matrix I think it's bullshit! It will only take a month or so!" Henry said.

They all gave him the finger.

C. D. Moulton's works are available on most major outlets as printed or e-books. CD writes the CD Grimes, PI, mysteries, the Det. Lt. Nick Storie mysteries, the Clint Faraday mysteries, the Flight of the Maita science fiction series, books on orchid culture and many others of many types. Mystery, adventure, intrigue, science fiction, humor, fantasy, paranormal, mild erotica, and factual.

www.ingramcontent.com/pod-product-compliance
Lightning Source LLC
Chambersburg PA
CBHW072205150726
48002CB00014B/1336